ERRATICALLY EPIC!

WRITTEN BY
ADAM WALLACE

ILLUSTRATED BY
JAMES HART

KRUEGER WALLACE
PRESS

Erratically Epic!
First published in the Year of the Dragonhunter, 2017
by
Krueger Wallace Press

Email: **wally@adam-wallace-books.com** or visit
www.kruegerwallacepress.weebly.com or visit
www.adam-wallace-books.com or visit
my friend Matt. He's really nice and will probably buy you a
present.

Designer/Typesetter: James Hart
Printed by Kindle Direct Publishing
Edited by Tex Calahoon

ISBN: 978-0-9944693-6-6

Cataloguing-in-Publication entry is available
From The National Library of Australia
http://catalogue.nla.gov.au

Do not stick this book in a tin of paint.
This book is not a lifesaver or a dog.

For all the school plays I was never chosen for
... because I never auditioned.
- Adam

To my grade 2 teacher and the play we
never played.
- James

Chapter 1

Acting on the stage is where people overcome their problems. At least, that's what everyone keeps telling me.

'I knew a guy who stuttered, but when he acted, his speech was perfect.'

'I knew a woman who had a twitch, but when she acted, the twitch was gone!'

'I knew a guy who had no legs, but when he acted he could walk! It was a miracle!'

That was my Uncle Marty. He believes in miracles. Once he told me that he saw a person who had been dead for **25** years walking down the street.

I told him that wasn't a miracle, that was a zombie.

He said not only was the person alive, but they had changed from a man to a woman and were 15 years younger than when they had died. I told him it was a totally different person, but he didn't listen. He just kept talking about other miracles. I let him keep going, until he told a story about a monkey that married a cheetah.

That freaked me out.

Anyway, I can't see how being on the stage is going to help me be less clumsy. I do acting classes though, and I guess it **would** be kind of cool to be a world-famous superstar actor.

Yeah, that would be awesome.

Sometimes, I imagine myself in all the great movies. I see myself in a zombie movie, and I'm the hero, and zombies are closing in on me, grunting and groaning and wanting to eat my brains. I throw things at them, but they just catch and eat them, and then I realise I had been throwing brains and that was really stupid because brains make zombies stronger and faster.

So then I pick up some other stuff and throw that, and they just catch and eat those things too, and I realise that everything I pick up and throw turns into a brain! **Whoops!** I turn and charge at the zombies, accidentally stand on a skateboard, skate up a ramp, crash into a display of samurai swords, the stand falls over, the swords chop off the zombies' heads, and they die … again.

Yep, even in my imagination I am erratically epic!

Then I might imagine myself in an action movie, and I'm the good guy, and these bad guys have taken over a building and are threatening to blow it up unless the Prime Minister pays them 45 billion dollars! **And I'm the Prime Minister!**

What the bad guys don't know is that, in this imaginary story, I'm also an expert in karate, boxing, ninjitsu, and line dancing. So I get my dad to be Prime Minister for the day while I take care of the bad guys. He's really happy about it, and gives everyone a day off work and free popcorn.

Jeez, Dad, way to be a dodgy Prime Minister.

Anyway, I go into the building and up the elevator. I get out at the top floor. All the bad guys are there, waiting for me. I run towards them doing a war cry. They shoot bows and arrows at me. I slip on a donut that one of them had left on the ground and as I fall I dodge all the arrows.

They **ooooh** and **ahhhh** and get scared because they thought I had done it on purpose. I confuse them by jumping up and doing some line dancing. One of them wants to join in, but the boss stops him.

I sneakily pick up a folder off a desk, and I wave around the folder as I dance … just as they throw hand grenades at me! The folder's like a tennis racquet! It hits the hand grenades back at the bad guys and blows them out the window.

Now that I've saved the day, I sack Dad because he had given a speech saying that if everyone voted for him he would make sure that the seats in cinemas had better cushions. Then I realise that's actually a really good point, so I let Dad be Prime Minister. Suddenly, the phone snapped me out of my dream world.

It was my best friend, Johnny, reminding me that auditions for the school play were on at five o'clock, and that if I was going to be a world-famous superstar actor, I needed to audition. It was already 4:45. I needed to get to school and I needed to get there **fast!** I hung up the phone, ran outside, picked up my bike, and rode off at full speed.

Chapter 2

I arrived at school at 5:10pm. I was sure that would be okay though. Mr Tee Tee was in charge of the school play, and he *really* likes me. I raced into the school theatre and saw heaps of people sitting in the seats waiting to audition. Up on stage was Teegan Wentworth, the prettiest, most awesome at acting, most legendary girl at school … if you like that sort of thing.

She was saying her whole audition without even reading it! It was **_AMAZING!!!_**

I went to sit down, but I didn't realise the seat was one of those theatre seats where you have to put them down first. I sat on it **without** putting it down, which made me bounce forward and I head-butted Mr Tee Tee in the back of the head. Not a good start to getting the main part.

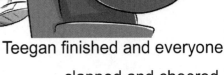

Teegan finished and everyone clapped and cheered. 'Excellent, Teegan,' said Mr Tee Tee, rubbing his head. He had a little microphone clipped to his top so everyone could hear him.

'Next person on the audition list is Barney Hippole.'

Barney waddled onto the stage. I'm not being mean, he actually *did* waddle. He was dressed in a penguin suit. I leant forward.

'Mr Tee Tee,' I whispered. 'I forgot to put my name down, but can I audition anyway?'

Mr Tee Tee shook his head, not realising I was so close, and we butted heads **again**.

'Sorry, Mr Tee Tee,' I said, leaning in even closer. 'I didn't mean to head-butt you, but I would really, **really** like to audition. Pretty please?'

Now. One problem with me is that when I say words that start with p, I tend to spit. Another problem was that Mr Tee Tee was just turning around to tell me to be quiet, so his mouth was open really wide. The final problem was a combination of the first two problems ... my spit went **straight into Mr Tee Tee's mouth.**

He coughed and gagged. Barney stopped doing his penguin tap dance and ran off the stage crying because he thought Mr Tee Tee was doing spew sounds at how bad he was.

Mr Tee Tee glared at me. 'Jackson Payne, if I let you audition will you leave me alone?'

I didn't realise that the microphone was still on. Otherwise I would *never* have said what I did.

'Of course, Mr Tee Tee. And I will never, **EVER** tell anyone that I just spat in your mouth. It's our little secret. Okay? Just between you and me and no-one else.'

Everyone started laughing. Mr Tee Tee slapped himself in the forehead.

'You audition last. Until then, you stay very still, okay?'

I nodded and accidentally head-butted him one more time. Even in the dark I could see him go red, so I quickly moved to the back row, sat in a seat, and waited to be a star of the stage.

Chapter 3

Johnny was the next person up to audition. Johnny's my best friend ever. We always sit next to each other in class, even when teachers say we shouldn't because we make each other laugh all the time. I was **really** excited to see what he would do.

Johnny walked out onto stage really slowly. He had on a mask that covered half his face. He had on a cape. He had asked for the lights to be turned down low, so that you could only sort of see him. It was all **very** mysterious. He walked to the centre of the stage.

Everyone leant forward, waiting. This was a whole different side to Johnny. I sat on the edge of my seat, wondering what would happen next.

Johnny stopped walking. He stared at the ground. Slowly, he looked up at the audience. We all held our breath. He dramatically raised one hand. He looked at the roof. He started to sing.

'Ohhhhh, I love to sing a farty song,
I love to fart fart all day long.
A day with no farts is a day with no cheeeeeer,
So here is what you've come to hear!'

And then he did - and I swear this is true, no lie, cross my heart and hope to live a long time - he did the **BIGGEST** pop-off you have **EVER** heard.

Everyone cracked up laughing, even Mr Tee Tee, although he stopped really quickly and told Johnny off for being rude. It was **SOOOO** funny. I ran back stage and found Johnny. We high-fived.

'How did you fart so loud?' I asked. 'Do you have a microphone taped to your butt?'

Johnny laughed and shook his head, then took something out of his pocket.

'Nope. Just my trusty **FaRT-O-MaTiC 3000**™ turned onto full power.'

Of course! The **FaRT-O-MaTiC 3000**™!
I should have known. Johnny never leaves home without it. One time he kept setting it off in a food court and then pointing to different people. So funny.

'Our last audition is, sigh, Jackson Payne,' I heard Mr Tee Tee say. I high-fived Johnny again and walked out onto the stage. As I walked past the curtain, my foot caught on a rope without me noticing.

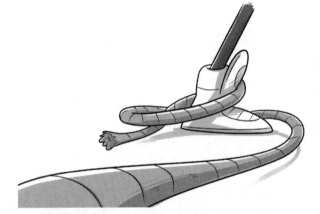

I kept walking and then suddenly the rope tightened like one of those traps in the jungle.

It swung me off my feet and the curtain started closing. I swung past the fake castle and knocked it over. I swung past a cardboard tree and smashed it in half.

I ended up hanging upside down. It was a bit scary, but kind of cool at the same time. I pretended I had meant it.

'Ladies, gentlemen, and Mr Tee Tee,' I said. Mr Tee Tee made a weird growling noise.

'I will now do my entire audition upside down,' I continued, 'even though my face is going red and I am starting to feel dizzy.'

'Jackson, would you like us to help you down?' Mr Tee Tee asked.

'Only if you want to ruin the greatest upside down audition ever,' I said. 'Prepare to be *amazed!*

I am going to do an entire scene from *Zombies Gone Wild*. I will be playing the parts of the zombies **and** the people whose brains they are trying to eat. Here goes.

Gaaaarrrrgggghhhh. ***HELP!*** Grrrrrrr, brains yum. ***Please help us. Screeeeeeaaaammmmm!*** Orrrrrgggggghhhh. ***I want my mummy.*** Brains. Must ... eat ... brains. ***Screeeeeeeeeaaaaaaaaaa mmmmmmmmmmm!*** Gaaaaarrrrrgggghhhhh chew chew munch munch swallow. Brains yum. And thank you.'

I did a hanging upside down bow. Everyone clapped. I saw Mr Tee Tee write something on his sheet.

'Thank you, Jackson, that was just what I expected.'

'Thanks, Mr Tee Tee,' I said. Mr Tee Tee continued.

'Here are the roles for the play. Teegan Wentworth will be playing Julie. Stevie J will be playing Roman. Johnny will be playing the court jester.'

He went on and on with all these other roles but didn't mention me. I was still hanging upside down and was feeling really dizzy now. Finally, Mr Tee Tee said my name.

'And Jackson Payne will be playing the role of the tree, replacing the cardboard one he has just broken.'

Everyone laughed, the rope went loose and I fell to the ground in a heap. It had *not* been a good audition.

Chapter 4

We had our first rehearsal the next day after school. It meant I missed out on watching after-school cartoons, but I didn't mind. Well, I **thought** I didn't mind, but then we had the actual rehearsal. Of all the **boring**, **dull**, **stupid** and **boring** things ever in the history of the world, this was the most boring, dull, stupid and boring **of them all.**

Mr Tee Tee made me stand at the back of the stage.

Then he told me to act like a tree. I waved my arms around and threw acorns at people. Mr Tee Tee hadn't quite moved out of the way though, so an acorn bonked off his head and I eye-gouged him pretty hard.

POKE!

He held my arms still and told me not to move from that position.

It was really hard! The tree was in almost every single scene, and I just had to stand still and not move. I didn't even have a costume yet, so it was just me standing there while everyone else got to say lines and jump around and do all sorts of cool stuff. Stevie J even got to swing on a rope!

Here's a list of things that happened while I was trying to stand still.

My nose got itchy.

My arms got pins and needles.

My butt got pins and needles.

I asked Mr Tee Tee if I could be
something else, because being
a tree was really boring.
He said no.
I *really* wanted to act with
Teegan Wentworth,
so I changed from a tree to a
creeper vine, and I crept over to where
Teegan was practicing. Mr Tee Tee saw me
though, and made me go back.
My butt got itchy again.
I started pulling *funny* faces at
Johnny. I started pulling *weird*
faces at Stevie J. I started pulling
scary faces at the little preppie kids who
were singing a song.

The little preppie kids
started crying.

I tried more funny faces,
but that was a bad move!

The little preppie kids cried even more and one of them peed his pants! Mr Tee Tee yelled at me. The preppie kids cried at me.

Our Principal, Mrs Frownface, I mean Mrs Townace, came into the theatre, asked what had happened, and then *she* yelled at me!

And that was only the first three minutes!

I stopped pulling faces, stuck my branches out and stood perfectly still, staring straight ahead. **SOOOO BORING!** I needed an excuse to get out of there.

I asked Mr Tee Tee if I could please go to the toilet. He said yes, so I walked off the stage, not realising that my shoelace was undone. I tripped over it and landed right on top of one of the little preppies. He started crying again. I picked him up and went to put him on a seat, but I missed and he fell onto his butt on the stage. He cried even louder!

I tried to help him, but it was just as he was standing up and I head-butted him and knocked him down *again*.

I decided to let him get up by himself.

I tied my shoelace and walked off. I was still watching the little preppie to make sure he was okay, which meant I walked right off the front of the stage and landed in the lap of the person sitting in the front row. It was Mrs Frownface. She grunted and pushed me off her lap.

'Sorry, Mrs Frow, I mean Mrs Townace,' I said.

'Jaaaaaackson Paaaaaayyyyne,' she said. Her words always went longer when she was angry. 'You are noooo longer a treeeeeeeeeee!'

'Awesome,' I said. 'Being a tree is **terrible**. What part have I got now?'

'Yoooooooooou are now a staaaaaaage hand,' Mrs Frownface said.

Mr Tee Tee ran over and tried to convince Mrs Frownface to change her mind. He couldn't. I didn't even really know what being a stagehand meant, but she sent me backstage to go and work with Markus Smith. **Backstage?** Suddenly, being a tree didn't look so bad after all. I had to work out a way to get from backstage back onto that stage.

Chapter 5

Markus Smith stood next to all the different things that had to go on stage during the show.

'This is a **REALLY** important job, Jackson,' he said.

I believed him too. Markus Smith is the smartest kid in our whole grade, so if he said it was important then it probably was.

'What do we have to do?' I asked.

'Every time something new, like a chair, or table, has to go on stage, *we* take it on.'

'Okay,' I said. Didn't sound too exciting.

'And every time someone needs a hat or cloak, *we* have to hand it to them.'

'Right.'

'And every time something has to come off the stage, *we* have to go out and get it.'

'Doesn't sound too hard,' I said.

Markus smiled.

'***And we have to do it all in between scenes when it is pitch black and we can't hardly see where we're going!***'

34

Now *that* sounded like *much* more fun than being a tree. I would get to be on stage, even though it would be so dark no-one could see me. I would also get to take things out for Teegan Wentworth, which would be pretty cool … if you like that sort of thing. And best of all, if I had an itchy butt I could scratch it, not like when I was a tree and had to be perfectly still. Just the thought of it gave me an itchy butt, so I scratched it … just as Teegan Wentworth walked backstage to ask for a favour from Markus.

Ah, bum.

Teegan giggled.

'Hope you haven't caught the acting bug, Jackson,' she said.

I laughed and stopped scratching my butt. Teegan asked Markus if he could take out an extra brush for the scene where she had to sit in front of the mirror talking about how she wished she could ride her horse more often. Markus said that was fine. Teegan left, and I asked Markus if *I* could take out that brush. He shrugged and said sure.

Then Markus gave me a piece of paper which listed every single thing we had to do, and when we had to do it. He told me not to lose or eat the paper, as it was **really** important.

We went through the list. At the end of the first scene we had to take on a table with candles on it. Things like that. It all looked pretty easy, and the best thing was that without us the show couldn't go on. **We were the most important people in the whole show.** I was going to be a star after all!

Chapter 6

We had three more rehearsals. I watched every one of them, and put all the right things on stage, and didn't fall over more than about five times. I also listened really carefully and knew almost all the lines in the show!

Then it was time for the big dress rehearsal. Mr Tee Tee had invited in some kids from school, and some teachers too, so that everyone could get used to performing in front of an audience.

I peeked out from behind the curtain and started to get nervous.

'Dude,' I said to Markus. 'There are a whole lot of people out there!'

He smiled.

'Don't worry about it, Jackson. We have the list. All you have to do is follow the list and we'll be fine. It's all about the list. *List. LIIIIIIIIIIST!*'

I smiled and let him go, but inside I was panicking.

THE LIST!

I remembered how, that very morning, Johnny had come over and we were mucking around and he dared me to put 12 pieces of paper in my mouth. I had screwed up all the paper and shoved it in, not realising until ***this very moment*** that the last piece of paper I shoved in had been sitting on my desk ...

... in the ***exact*** spot that I had left the list of backstage duties.

That's because it ***was*** the list of backstage duties!

I had shoved it in my mouth, Johnny had cheered, and then I had spat all the paper out into our big yellow recycling bin.

Uh-oh.

I tried to remember everything I had to do, but my mind was a blank. Well, not exactly a blank, but all that was in my head was a monkey riding a horse, and that was not helpful at all … it *was* funny though!

I thought about telling Markus, but I knew he only had one sheet and we had to be on opposite sides of the stage. I *also* knew he would be disappointed in me, because he had said to me that the sheet of paper was the single most important thing for a backstage person, and I had to make absolutely sure that I didn't lose it or eat it. I had thought he had been joking about the eating it thing. Now I knew better.

This was a *disaster*. I started to panic. I stood at the side of the stage and looked at all the props. I had done this so many times, surely I could remember what I had to do once we got started.

Surely.

The show started, everyone in the audience cheered, and Billy Silver started speaking. Then Johnny came on and did all this funny stuff, the audience laughed, and the first scene ended.

I just stood there. I froze. I could not remember what to do.

'PSSSSST!'

I looked over and saw Markus on the other side of the stage.

'*Table*,' he whispered really loudly.

Of course! The table with the candle on it! I got really excited and picked up the table and ran onto the stage. I skidded to a stop and put the table down then slammed the candlestick on top of it. I turned to leave. The candlestick wobbled. I turned back. It stopped wobbling. I turned away, knocked the candle and sent it flying. It was still pitch black.

The candlestick landed on the stage with a *MASSIVE* clang. I got down on my hands and knees but it was nowhere to be seen. Suddenly the lights came on and there I was, crawling around the stage searching.

IT'S BEHIND YOU!

I turned around, but when I did I kicked the candlestick off the stage. It landed in Mrs Townace's coffee and splashed coffee all over her. She became Mrs Frownface for real. I ran offstage and hoped things would get better.

Things didn't get better. Here's a short run-down of what happened during the rehearsal, taking out all the yelling and everything that everyone did.

1. I took out Teegan Wentworth's brush *eight* times. Not once was it actually the *right* time. She was really nice about it though, and by the eighth time she had the shiniest, most brushed hair ever!

2. Instead of taking out school bags for the preppies, who were acting as school-kids, I took out sandbags, which were used to weigh things down.

None of the preppies could even lift them.

3. I *did* remember to take out the fake exercise weights, but got so excited that I forgot to tighten up the ends, so when Stevie J lifted them they all fell off and rolled off the stage.

4. I closed the curtain right when the most important scene in the whole play started.

5. I threw raw eggs instead of rice during the wedding scene. I panicked and grabbed the next thing I could and threw that.

It was golden syrup. *Why was that even there?*

I grabbed the next thing.

It was flour!

Where was I, in a restaurant?

6. At one point, all the actors were on stage. It was pitch black. Markus and I had to go on and put flowers on the ground around them, so that when the lights came on it would look like the flowers had grown. Markus did it perfectly. I don't know how. When I tried it was an ***absolute disaster!***

Turn the page for a full description ...

I stepped on Johnny's toe, I elbowed Stevie J in the tummy, I put flowers down one kid's top, I tripped over the fake watering hose, and I pulled over three people! They grabbed three *other* people, and we all ended up crashing to the ground and lying in the fake pond.

The lights went up.

'*JAAAAAACCCKKKKSSSOOONNNNNN PAAAAAAAYYYYYYYYYYYNNNNNNE!!!*'

Uh-oh.

That was the longest Mrs Frownface had **ever** taken to say my name. I was in SOOOOOOOOOOOOOO much trouble.

Chapter 7

I got kicked out of the school play. I had really started enjoying being part of it too, so I wasn't happy. I asked if I could even be an usher or something, but Mr Tee Tee said no. So I was gone. No more being a tree. No more backstaging. No more nothing … actually, **lots** more nothing.

I wandered out of rehearsal, got my bike, and started riding slowly home. As I went, I heard someone yell out, 'Left!'

I turned left, looked right and fell down, taking the someone with me in a pile of arms, legs, wheels and leg warmers. It was Nan, out for her afternoon power walk. She had weights on her wrists and ankles, and leg warmers over her ankles too. She looked like an aerobics instructor from the land that time forgot.

'Sorry, Nan,' I said as I helped her up.

I turned to get on my bike but missed and fell over.

'Jackson,' Nan said. 'That isn't how you get onto a bike ... actually, it really is! But is something wrong? You look sad.'

'No,' I said.

'Do you mean yes?' Nan asked.

'No,' I said, nodding.

Nan said we should go and sit on the sit-up bench that was by the path, so I followed her over.

Then I held her feet while she did twenty sit-ups.

'Okay Jackson, spit it out,' Nan said.

I spat out the chewing gum I was chewing. Nan slapped her forehead.

'No, Jackson, the story. Spit out what's wrong with you.'

Oh. Right. I told Nan everything then, about how I had auditioned for the school play, how I had thought I would be a world-famous superstar actor, but how I had been cast as a tree, got kicked backstage, and then had wrecked the whole dress rehearsal.

I told her how good Teegan Wentworth was, and how good Johnny was, and how I couldn't even be a tree. I had thought maybe being an actor might stop me being so clumsy, but it just felt like I was even more clumsy than ever.

Nan looked at me for what seemed like ages.

I stared back for a bit, but I was looking so closely I could see little bits of gunk in the corner of her eyes.

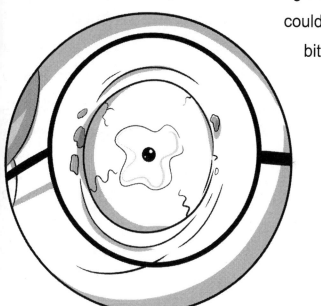

That totally grossed me out so I very politely looked away.

'I don't know, Jackson,' Nan suddenly said, sighing. I thought she was disappointed in me.

'Sorry, Nan,' I said.

'No,' Nan said. 'I wasn't saying I don't know about you, I was saying **I don't know**. I can't work this one out. I don't know what the lesson is here. It's a mystery.'

I felt really bad. Nan always tried so hard to help me, and it always took me ages to understand what she meant. This time, I decided I would use my acting skills to pretend I knew what she was talking about.

'Of **course**, Nan. You're a **genius**. The play's a mystery, so I just need to solve the mystery and everything will be okay.'

'No, that's not what I'm saying, Jackson. I actually don't know what to tell you here. It truly is a conundrum.'

I didn't know what sort of drum a conun drum was, but there *was* a drum in the play.

'The drum,' I said, getting excited. 'Of *course*. That would be perfect, Nan.'

'Jackson,' Nan said, 'listen to me. I don't think there's a lesson to be learned here. It may just be a situation with no message, no moral.'

I kept up with my acting.

'You are spot on, Nan, that is exactly what I'll do.'

'I didn't tell you to do anything.'

'And by doing that you told me to do everything!' I yelled. 'You are seriously the best. It's like watching a play!'

Watching a play? Suddenly, I started to *actually* get an idea. I would go and watch the play and support everyone, even though I wasn't in it anymore.

It was *genius!*

'No no no no *no*,' Nan said. 'You don't understand. No message. No lesson. This just is.'

'Just is the best advice you've ever given me is what it is!' I yelled. 'It's like we're two people but with the one brain.'

'Sometimes I think there *is* one brain between us,' Nan sighed. 'Let this one go, Jackson.'

'Oh, I'll go, Nan. I'll go for *glory!* Nan, we are tuned in to the same station. 103.4 FM, Nan and Jackson Legendaryness.'

'I can't do this anymore, Jackson, you're not even listening.'

'Or am I listening so well that I'm hearing things you're not even saying? Am I hearing messages on the 12th dimension of this conversation? Is my listening so good that it's like a whistle that only a dog can hear, and you're the whistle, and I'm the dog? I'm one of those tough dogs, by the way, not a wimpy little yappy one.'

Nan stood up.

'I have to go, Jackson. Move on from this, your next adventure will be upon you soon.'

'That's right, Nan, the adventure at the play.'

Nan stared at me. I gave her the thumbs up.

'You're a dull boy, Jackson,' she said, before walking off, swinging her arms as she went.

She really was a great Nan, and I was convinced of two things. One, I could definitely act. I had really put on an awesome show for Nan. Two, I needed to go and watch the play. I had to be a great friend to Johnny, and I had to show Mr Tee Tee that I could be a good audience member, even if I was a lousy tree.

I got back on my bike and sped off towards home. I had to convince Mum and Dad to take me to the school play.

Chapter 8

'Pleeeeeeeeeeeeeeeeeeeeeeeeeeeeeeeeease, Mum?   Pleeeeeeeeeeeeeeeeeeeeeeeeeeeeeease, Dad?'

I was trying a new tactic. Usually I would ask Mum and Dad hundreds of times until they gave in, but I didn't have time for that. So instead I asked in a really whiny, annoying voice that would drive them so crazy they would have to say yes. That was my theory anyway.

Okay then, so much for that theory.

'We're sorry, Jackson,' Mum said, 'but Mrs Frow, I mean Mrs Townace said you were banned from going to the play. You are not allowed in that theatre until the play is finished.'

'She actually said to me I wasn't allowed in there until I was 45 years old.'

Dad smiled.

'I negotiated for you, son. All those years of watching lawyer shows on TV have turned me into a master negotiator.'

Sure Dad, okay, either way it wasn't going to help me right now.

'But what if I sit with you guys?' I asked. 'Then you can both make sure that I don't do anything except go in, sit down, watch the play, support my friends, and leave. Huh? *HUH?*'

Mum and Dad looked at each other. Then they looked at me. Then they looked at each other again. Dad turned to me first.

'I'll give it a try, Jackson. I don't know how my negotiating skills will go over the phone, though.

Still, there's only one way to find out. It's time for Mr Charm to lay on the charmy charm like a super charmy charmer.'

He picked up the phone, looked up a number and dialed. Mum and I watched. This was Dad's side of the conversation.

'Hello Mrs Frow, I mean Mrs Townace,' Dad said. 'Sorry to bother you at home, but I was hoping to ask you a favour. It's about Jackson and the play.'

'I know that, but he's a good boy at heart. And I know you are too, Mrs T.'

'No, I won't ever call you that again, I'm sorry.'

'Yes.'

'We just thought he could …'

'Yes.'

'No.'

'What if he …'

'I understand, but I have one last thing to say, and I hope you will listen 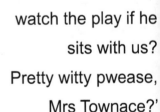 and consider my argument carefully. Pleeeeeeeeeeeeeeeeease can Jackson come and watch the play if he sits with us? Pretty witty pwease, Mrs Townace?'

Wow, Dad. Really? I'm pretty sure no TV lawyer in the history of TV has **EVER** used *that* technique!

Suddenly though, Dad's eyes lit up.

'Really? That actually **worked?** That's amazing. Thank you so much, Mrs Frow, I mean Mrs Townace, you are such a darling sweetheart … no, I will never say that again either. Thank you. Good bye. Nighty night, sleep tight … sorry. Bye now.'

Dad hung up the phone then looked at us.

'You're in, Jackson. We're going to the school play!'

WOO HOO!!!

I ran over and hugged Dad. What a champion. Sure, it may have taken him whining like a little baby to get results, but he had done it and he had done it for me. The Paynes were going to the school play.

Chapter 9

The night of the play arrived. I dressed up in my good jeans and shirt, and off we went. We were sitting in the back row, but that was okay. It was a pretty good view from up there. The curtain was down, but I could see it rustling and I could hear voices behind it.

Something was wrong.

I looked past Dad and saw that Mrs Frownface was sitting just a few seats down from us. Suddenly, Mr Tee Tee squeezed past people and started whispering to her. I leant over, but I couldn't quite hear. I leant a little further.

My head rested on Dad's popcorn. My ear started to smell like butter, but at least I could hear. 'He can't play the role,' Mr Tee Tee whispered. 'What role?' I asked. They both looked around.

'Don't eavesdrop, Jackson,' Dad said, but Mr Tee Tee was looking at me. So was Mrs Frownface.

'Do you know the play, Jackson?' Mr Tee Tee asked.

'Every word,' I said, sitting up straight and knocking Dad's popcorn out of his hands and all over the person in front of him. Mrs Frownface shook her head and rubbed her eyes. Then she breathed deep and looked at Mr Tee Tee.

'Okay, Marmaduke, but it's on your head. If Jackson ruins the stage it comes out of your pay.'

Marmaduke? Mr Tee Tee's name was Marmaduke??? Oh, this was the **best!** Mr Marmaduke Tee Tee nodded, then looked at me. 'Come on, Jackson,' he said, 'we have to get you into costume.'

'Yes, Marmaduke, I mean Mr Tee Tee,' I said, trying not to giggle.

I stood up and ran out of the aisle, stepping on a toe or two as I went. I didn't care. I was so excited, and not just about the play.

Mr Tee Tee's name was Marmaduke!

69

Mr Tee Tee led me backstage. Everyone looked really stressed. There, lying on the ground, was Billy Silver. Billy was the narrator. He had to introduce the play, do some little bits during it, and then close the whole thing at the end.

Unfortunately, Billy had eaten a whole bunch of rotten baked beans, and had the smelliest case of ... it wasn't even food poisoning, it was more like fart poisoning. It smelt *rotten*. Billy's parents took him off to the car. I hoped they had gas masks in there.

I got dressed in the narrator's costume, which was jeans and a shirt. That was what I was already wearing, but these were special ones. Suddenly, I got really nervous. I started sweating, and got a lump in my throat. Johnny raced up to me.

'Dude!' he said. 'We're in a play together! How cool is this?'

It was **very** cool, but I seemed to have forgotten how to speak. I tried to sit in a chair but missed and sat in a bucket, which stuck on my butt. Mr Tee Tee pulled it off and put it aside. Then he sighed and wished me luck. I was so nervous and I really needed to pee! But I had to go and start the play. To pee or not to pee, that was the question!

I didn't have time to answer it though, as I got pushed out onto the stage. It was showtime. The curtain went up and a spotlight turned on, making it hard for me to see.

I took a step towards the front of the stage and tripped over a cable. I flipped forward, did a full somersault, and landed on my feet. I hadn't meant it, but the crowd cheered. Now it was time to speak.

'Be – be – be – be be –'

I couldn't get the words out. Acting hadn't cured me of a stutter, *it had given me one!*

I was **SO** scared.

I stared side-stage, and Johnny gave me the thumbs-up. That relaxed me. Then Teegan Wentworth smiled and nodded. That relaxed me too. Then I looked out at the audience and saw

Mum and Dad watching, and I wanted to do well for them.

I heard people in the audience start whispering to each other, so I needed to do something. I took a massive breath, and then spoke in my loudest voice.

'BE – BE – BE – *BEFORE!*'

Everyone stopped muttering and I breathed a sigh of relief.

I was back.

'Before we begin, I must ask you to turn off your mobile phones. I must ask you to turn off your radios. I must ask you to turn up your hearing aids. You too, Mrs Townace.'

I threw that last bit in … it's called improvising. Everyone laughed, so that was good. Mrs Frownface frowned, so that was bad, although not really surprising. I went back to the script and finished off the introduction speech.

'This play is not for a certain few. This play is for all manner of people. Rude people, polite people, it is for everyone. Even you, Mrs Townace.'

Everyone cracked up. I was on a roll. Mrs Frownface looked like she wanted to eat me for breakfast.

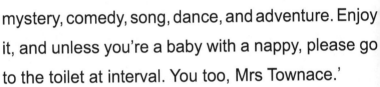

I finished things up.

'This is a play of mystery, comedy, song, dance, and adventure. Enjoy it, and unless you're a baby with a nappy, please go to the toilet at interval. You too, Mrs Townace.'

Then I turned to run offstage, but forgot that while I was speaking some of the others had come out, so I turned and ran straight into Johnny, and we both fell into the pram that was behind him.

'Waaaaaah,' we cried, and everyone laughed. Then Johnny, what an acting star, got out and pushed me offstage in the pram. I waved. Everyone cheered, and the play began.

I got out of the pram when we were out of view. Mr Tee Tee was there. He grabbed me by the shoulders. I thought he was going to yell at me for making jokes at Mrs Townace, but he didn't. He just smiled and gripped my shoulders. 'Wonderful,' he said. 'Really?' I asked. He nodded, patted my shoulders, and then walked off. *That* was pretty cool.

I stood in the wings with Johnny when he wasn't acting and we watched the show. It was *really* good. Teegan Wentworth was awesome. So was everyone else. The audience laughed when we wanted them to, and cheered the good guys, and booed the bad guys. Then, at one point, all the actors came off the stage. I was having a drink. I stood and watched, wondering what was meant to be happening. Was it interval already? No, there was one more thing before the interval. Billy had to close out the – uh-oh. ***I was being Billy tonight!***

I raced onto the stage, forgetting I was still holding my drink. I stumbled on the leg of a table and almost dropped the drink. I juggled it for a bit, all the time nearly falling over because I was right on the edge of the stage.

Then Johnny saved me again. He's **such** a good friend. He came out juggling some balls, because he was the jester and everything, and he could actually juggle. He juggled up to me and caught the drink and started juggling that, and I spoke.

Yep. I only had one line there, but it was an important one!

The curtain came down just as Johnny dropped the drink and it went all over a lady in the front row. Everyone cheered, thinking it was part of the act and that the drink was really some sort of special theatre liquid that would just wash out.

They were wrong.

Whoops.

The rest of the night passed in a blur. I introduced the second half, the actors all did their thing, and then I had to close the show. Johnny pushed me out in the pram.

'Ladies and gentlemen,' I said. 'Thank you for coming into our world tonight. We hope you enjoyed the play, and we hope that you drive home safely.

Especially you, Mrs Townace.'

'Awwwwwwwww,' everyone awwwwwwwwed. I got out of the pram and finished up.

'Thank you, and goodnight!'

We all held hands and bowed. Everyone cheered. We bowed again, but I went a bit far and started to fall. I tried to stand up again, but I couldn't.

I pulled down the person next to me, they pulled the person next to them, and we went over like a row of dominoes. The curtain closed for the last time and the crowd gave us a standing ovation.

We all lay on the ground laughing like crazy. Mr Tee Tee said it was the best school play we'd *ever* had, and that even Mrs Townace was clapping and cheering at the end.

I couldn't stop smiling!

Teegan Wentworth came up and gave me a hug and said I was her hero for saving the show. It was **EPiC**, and that's a wrap!

ABOUT THE AUTHOR

Adam Wallace writes a letter to Santa every year, and puts out a Christmas stocking every year. This is partly because it makes his mum excited, and partly because it makes him **REALLY** excited.

Adam loves spending Christmas with his favourite people, and he loves eating fruit salad.

He doesn't like eating Christmas pudding, because he's allergic to some things in it and he hates that gross fake fruit stuff.

Find out more about Adam
at www.adam-wallace-books.com

ABOUT THE ILLUSTRATOR

James Hart is an illustrator, character designer & comic artist that has worked with many companies and clients worldwide since 2003. His work has appeared in books, magazines, websites, posters, comics, and on TV as a character and prop designer for shows such as *Sumo Mouse* and *The Day My Butt Went Psycho!*

He currently lives on the Mornington Peninsula in Victoria, Australia with his wife and kids.

Find out more about James
at www.jameshart.com.au

OTHER BOOKS BY ADAM WALLACE

and

JAMES HART!

Cowboy and Birdbrain: Don't say the P word

Cowboy and Birdbrain: POOP of DOOM

Fartboy: The First Sniff

Fartboy: Ready, Aim, FART!

Fartboy: Enter the Spewtank

'Twas the Fart Before Christmas

Zombie Inspiration

Ninja Inspiration

And, of course, all the other books in the Jackson Payne series, which you can see on the following pages!

also available

also available

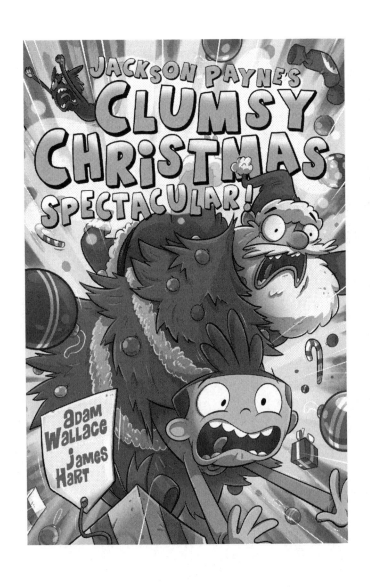

also available

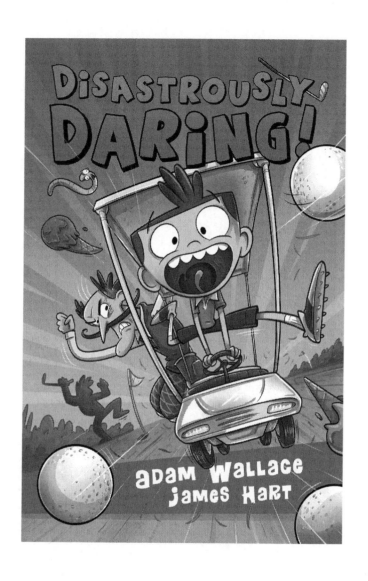

also available

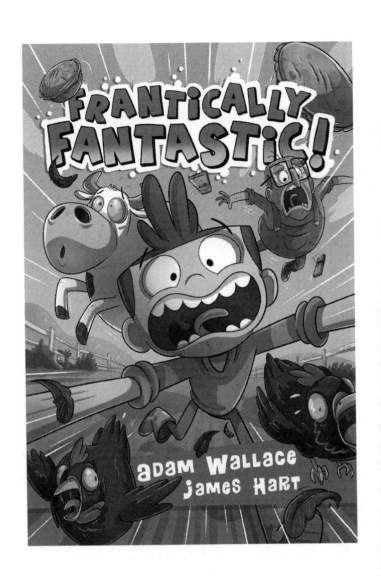

aLSO avaiLabLe

BE EPIC!

Made in the USA
Columbia, SC
22 January 2021